ISLINGTON LIBRARIES

D0490223

This book belongs to:

...............................................................

...............................................................

Love you Chloe & Ben.
It is a long time since your first day of school,
but our love for you gets bigger everyday.
Mum & Dad

Editor: Sophie Hallam
Designer: Michael Henson
Editorial Director: Victoria Garrard
Art Director: Laura Roberts-Jensen

Copyright © QED Publishing 2015
First published in the UK in 2015 by QED Publishing

Part of The Quarto Group
The Old Brewery
6 Blundell Street
London N7 9BH
www.qed-publishing.co.uk

All rights reserved. No part of this publication may be reproduced, stored
in a retrieval system, or transmitted in any form or by any means, electronic,
mechanical, photocopying, recording, or otherwise, without the prior
permission of the publisher, nor be otherwise circulated in any form of
binding or cover other than that in which it is published and without a
similar condition being imposed on the subsequent purchaser.

A catalogue record for this book is available from
the British Library.

ISBN 978 1 78493 244 2

Printed in China

# Little Hedgehog's Big Day

## Daniel and Heidi Howarth

"Only a few days
to go until you
start big school!"
said Mum.

Little Hedgehog smiled. He knew Mum was
excited so he pretended he was too...

...but really his
tummy felt full
of butterflies.

That night Little Hedgehog was too worried to sleep...

He kept thinking about how big BIG SCHOOL would be.

Would there be a big table?

Would there be a **big** chair?

Would there be a **big** teacher?!

In the morning he knew
what he needed to do...

He had to get big,

**really BIG!**

But how?

"Exercise!"
said Rabbit.

"I bounce at least a hundred times a day.
It makes me strong and my legs long."

Rabbit stretched out his big bunny leg and Little Hedgehog compared it to his own. His looked tiny.

"Oh and I eat carrots... lots and lots of carrots," Rabbit said before bouncing away.

"Oh no," said Squirrel, "jumping makes you big. And eating nuts... lots and lots of nuts."

"They make me strong!" he said, flexing his muscles.

"See?" He jumped up quickly and dangled from a branch.

Little Hedgehog jumped but there was no way he could reach!

"Stretching," yawned Badger.
"I get bigger every time I stretch."

Little Hedgehog stretched
next to Badger but it just
made him feel even smaller.

So Little Hedgehog tried to bounce like Rabbit...

...jump like Squirrel...

...and stretch like Badger.

But he **still** didn't feel any bigger.

"What are you doing?"
asked Ant.

"I need to be big,"
cried Little Hedgehog,
"for big school!"

"Why?" said Ant. "I'm small but
I can still do lots of things!"

When he got home,
Little Hedgehog ran
to find his mum.

"Do you think I am ready for big
school?" he asked her.

"Well," she replied
thoughtfully,
"let's have a look."

She took down a photo
album from the shelf.

Inside were lots of photos of Little Hedgehog.

"Just look at all the things you have
done already," said Mum proudly.

Then Mum showed him an old picture
of a little hedgehog, with a school cap
and a shiny satchel.

"Goodness, that was my first day at school!"
said Dad from the doorway.

On the first day of school, Little Hedgehog was all ready to go.

"I look just like you, Dad!"
he said, smiling.

Little Hedgehog went to school
and it wasn't so big after all!

He took out his book and was just
practising his letters when...

"Wow," said Badger. "Can you show us?" they all asked together.

"Of course I can," he smiled. "I can do lots of things!"

# Next steps

Look at the cover of the book together. What is Little Hedgehog wearing? Do the children remember their first day at school, or are they starting school very soon?

Anything new can be a little bit scary. Everyone has felt 'butterflies' in their tummy when faced with a new place, new people or a new experience. Take this opportunity to talk to the children about school. Were they excited to be going? Or nervous, like Little Hedgehog? What were they excited or worried about?

Talk about the story. Little Hedgehog is worried – what does he try and do to solve his worries? What makes Little Hedgehog feel better in the end?

Little Hedgehog realizes all the things he can do which make him feel really big inside. What talents do the children have? What do they like to do?

In the story, Little Hedgehog is shown a book of photographs. Have the children ever seen pictures of themselves or their parents when they were younger? Have they ever seen any very old photographs of their families? If you can, print out some photos to help the children make their own photo album or draw a family tree.